Jane Hurley

A Woman Named Coral

A Woman Named Coral

a novel by JANE HUXLEY

DELANCEY PRESS
LONDON 2014

Published by Delancey Press Ltd
23 Berkeley Square
London W1J 6HE

www.delanceypress.co.uk
Copyright © Jane Huxley 2014

A CIP catalogue record for this title is available from the
British Library.

First published 2014
Painting by Peregrine Heathcote
Jacket by Michal William
Typeset by BookType
Printed and bound in Great Britain by TJ International Ltd

ISBN 978-1-907205-23-1

In memory of
Dame Beryl Bainbridge DBE

In her arms I tasted the delights of Paradise, and they produced these hellish torments by which you see me devoured.

Candide
VOLTAIRE

Torments that proclaim the approach of ecstasy, which none of us would willingly renounce.

J. H.

CONTENTS

ONE

An Enigmatic Question

S he opened her eyes to a slice of sun flickering on the pillow.

"Tom," she groaned. "Please close the shutters. I'm trying to sleep."

There was no answer from the other side of the bed. A vague Vétiver-scented haze from Tom's pillow pervaded the air. A moment later her husband's loud baritone bellowed from down-stairs.

"Missy, are you awake? Come down! You'll never guess who's here."

She knew at once it was her stepson, gorgeous Stefan, whose name alone suggested he was intriguing and adventurous – a sailor dangling from the mast of a storm-tossed ship.

"Coming," she sang, as she slipped into the

bathroom, brushed her hair and inspected her face, lips and almost transparent black négligé.

"Hello, darling," she said, as she offered him her cheek.

Stefan brushed it with his lips and his green eyes twinkled with amusement as they paused on the seductive hand placed across the breasts of his father's wife.

Irresistible, Missy thought, gazing at the eyes, the perfect patrician nose, and those sensual lips that suggested a perpetual craving for a kiss.

"Straight from Kabul," Tom announced, "where he had been sent by The Daily Telegraph."

As a freelance journalist, Stefan spent most of his time in remote parts of the world, which he laughingly explained as a way to escape the drab English winter.

"Coffee and croissants," Tom announced, as Missy set three places at the kitchen table. A moment later he addressed his son in a voice that was a trifle uncertain, "You want to tell her, or shall I?"

"Tell me what?" Missy asked.

"There has been another sighting," Tom said.

Missy looked at him, then at Stefan, as if she thought the comment was absurd.

The so-called "sighting" referred to the lost

daughter of Tom's friends, the Harringtons, who had died almost twenty years earlier in a mudslide in the northern province of Ancash, in Perú.

Their bodies had been recovered days after the avalanche, but that of their six-year old daughter had never been found. There was something hopeful and pathetic about the rumours and "sightings" that sprouted from various different sources from time to time.

"Another sighting?" Missy asked in a bored voice.

"This one is different." Tom said.

"In what way?"

"The source," Tom told her. "Professor Greene, a friend of the Harringtons, has met the young woman in Lima."

"What is she like?"

"Blond and beautiful, which is most unusual if her parents are brown skinned Indians from the Sierra."

"Strange story," Missy said.

"But life goes on," Tom explained. "The girl is now in her late twenties and married to a prominent member of Peruvian society."

"So," Missy concluded. "All's well that ends well."

"Hasn't ended yet," Tom said. "In fact, it has barely begun."

Missy turned to her stepson, who was drinking

his coffee and eating his second croissant. "What do you think of all this?" she asked.

"Don't know," he said. "May be worth trying to find out."

"Which is exactly what's going to happen," Tom said. "Because Stefan is going to Perú, on assignment from The New York Times."

"What a strange coincidence," Missy blurted.

"Not really," Stefan said. "I'm doing a piece on San Marcos University. While I'm there, I don't mind looking up Professor Greene, who has given Father this information."

"Oh, dear," Missy sighed. "With men the only way to win the battle is to agree with their most preposterous whims." A brief pause before she continued, "But, anyway, will you stay and have lunch with us?"

"I'm afraid I can't," Stefan said. "I'm expected in Hampstead. Mother wants to see me before I go to Perú."

"Dear Frances," Missy said, with a reptilian smile. "Give her my best, will you?"

TWO

Questions without Answers

Frances had always been an excellent cook and her favourite guest, her son Stefan, was sitting at the luncheon table, a bowl of *bouillabaisse* in front of him.

"Mother," he exclaimed. "This is better than Maxim's."

"Do they make *bouillabaisse* at Maxim's?" she asked, surprised.

"I don't know; but if they do, yours is better."

"Eat as much as you want. You need to put on some weight."

"Kabul is not the ideal place for it. I must say, I was happy to arrive, but a lot happier to leave."

They went on eating and after a while, Stefan's eyes paused on his mother's face. Still beautiful, despite the shadows under the eyes, the pinched mouth that used to be always smiling, and the grey strands of hair whose existence he had only recently noticed.

"Mother," he said, "you remember your friends, the Harringtons, don't you?"

"Of course, darling. How could I forget them? Keith and Margo, and their beautiful little daughter, Coral."

"Can you tell me what you remember about them?"

"Keith was an explorer, intent on finding an Inca tombstone in the northwest province of Ancash. Margo was a loving wife who found ancient ruins as interesting as a pile of mud. Their little daughter was delighted to be a part of the adventure."

Frances lowered her head, as if she were unwilling to rake among the ashes of her memory. Through the dining room window she could see two swans gliding on the pond beyond her garden.

"I'm sorry if your memories cause you sorrow," Stefan said, "but, as you know, there has been a sighting. What you tell me may make a difference between finding this young woman and not finding her."

"I understand," Frances said, and went on, "When the Harringtons announced their travel plans, both your father and I offered to keep the little girl with us in London until their return."

"But they declined?"

"They were unwilling to part from her, which we certainly understood."

"So they took off and…"

"…and were killed in the avalanche."

"Father told me. Awful story."

Frances removed the empty bowls of *bouillabaise* and brought a tray of cheese and biscuits.

"The bottom line is Coral," she said. "Twenty years later."

"Father said that she was raised by an Indian couple from the Sierra."

"That's correct. They spoke only *Quechua*, but they sent her to a bilingual school and encouraged her to learn Spanish and English.

"What, exactly, do you know about her?"

"Not much. That she's young, intelligent and very beautiful."

"What about him?"

"His name is Aurelio Fernandez-Concha. He's in his sixties, attractive, charismatic, and one of the wealthiest cotton growers in South America."

"A perfect match," Stefan said, with a touch of irony.

"You may not know this," Frances said. "But most everything in life is an exchange."

"Not very reassuring, is it? But, anyway, going back to Mr. Fernandez-Concha, I believe I can get an introduction from Professor Greene."

"That would certainly open doors and may provide some clues. At the moment all we have are questions without answers."

Stefan helped himself to a biscuit and a slice of Brie topped with a drop of honey.

"Sorry to impose this burden on you," Frances said.

"Not at all. I'll be glad to do what I can."

"Thank you, darling. I suppose this confirms that parents are needy."

Stefan laughed. A funny word. Needy. And yet, it brought to mind an image that was just the opposite – that of a heart of gold.

THREE

A Not so Pleasant Outing

April was Coral's favourite month. Though the hot Peruvian summer was over, the air was still warm, and the beauty of the trees, the hills and the sea seemed to keep body and soul in tune with one another. In April, she thought, you pretend to do as you're told, while doing exactly as you like.

What she liked was to ride up the steep hills, through the plains and around the plantation, faster and faster, on the magnificent horse her husband had given her as a gift.

"There is no other horse like you, Monsieur Brown," she shouted to him, as he jumped over a fence and bolted straight towards the pine trees he knew would lead to the creek.

That was when they heard the shots.

Monsieur Brown gave a frightened neigh and

raised himself on his hind legs so violently Coral would have been thrown off had she not been such an expert rider.

"Whoa," she said. "Whoa, Monsieur Brown. Nothing to be frightened about."

She slipped off the horse and tied him to a tree. "You stay here," she said. "I'm going to find out what's going on."

She saw Silvio watching her as she approached. He addressed her in a tone of apology. "Didn't frighten you, did I?"

"Of course not," Coral said. "Just wondered who was shooting and why."

He put down his rifle and looked at her with a grin. "The most beautiful woman in Perú," he said. "And she happens to be my father's wife."

The trees were utterly still. No breeze fluttered the leaves on their long branches. After a moment he addressed her again.

"Beautiful," he repeated, staring at the thick blond hair she had braided behind her back; her eyes, blue as a midnight sky; her sensuous lips.

"You have a very attractive wife, Silvio," she told him.

"Do I?"

"Not only attractive but seven months pregnant with your first child."

"So what?"

"Is that all you have to say?"

"That's not all. I want to know about you."

"Me?"

"Don't you ever crave a strong naked male between your thighs?"

Coral moved away stiffly. Within Silvio's tight khaki pants, she could see the bulk of his erection, sheathed in dust-coloured cloth.

"I ought to be getting back," she said.

"Don't be in such a hurry. You just got here."

"I'm off," she told him, and walked away.

"Coral, wait!" he yelled.

But she was already running away. The thought of their conversation was not only distasteful but threatening. It warned her what his intentions were and how far he might go to fulfill them.

She untied the horse and mounted with impatience. "Let's go, Monsieur Brown," she said. "Let's get the hell out of here."

As they rushed through the plains, she caught sight of a woman kneeling behind a clump of trees, half-hidden by the tall grasses.

"Whoa, Monsieur Brown," she yelled. "I think I know who that is."

She dropped down to the ground and ran towards the woman.

"Josefa," she shouted. "Is that you?"

It was indeed Josefa, her maid, who had served her breakfast a few hours earlier. What had happened between then and now that caused Josefa to kneel on the grass and shiver convulsively, her arms covering her head.

"Josefa," she cried. "What on earth is the matter?"

As she knelt beside her, she saw a pair of knitting needles and a lot of blood and blood clots on the ground.

"What is it?" Coral cried. "What has happened to you?"

"It's over," Josefa said. "I had to do what I did, and now it's over."

Coral understood. She took the maid in her arms and craddled her gently. Her voice was urgent but soft. "I can see what has happeened," she said. "But why? Why didn't you want this baby? Was it Rocco's baby?"

"No."

"Whose baby was it?"

Josefa just shook her head. She trembled and wept as Coral held her, clasping her arms closely around her.

"You can tell me," Coral said. "I only want to help you. I don't want any harm to come to you."

"The *señor*," Josefa mumbled, still crying.

"Who?"

"The *señor*," she repeated.

"What? My husband?" Coral exclaimed.

"No. No. Not your husband. It was *señor* Silvio who raped me. He said he'd kill me if I told anybody."

Coral held the woman with a mixture of pity and rage.

"You're going to be alright, Josefa," she said. "I'll get Dr. Martinez to come to the house. He is very kind and he will make sure you'll be fine. No one will ever know. Not Rocco. Not my husband. Not Silvio. No one. Just Dr. Martinez. And you and me."

Josefa put her arms around Coral and held her tightly.

FOUR

Of Love and Money

Aurelio Fernandez-Concha had always been wealthy and his wife, Carlota, was far wealthier than himself.

"Money attracts money," she had said to him when he had proposed to her.

He had replied, "But I love you."

"I never said you didn't," she had said, with a grin.

There was nothing beautiful about Carlota except her eyes, which were dark and vivacious. Her nose was too long, her mouth too small, her body too scrawny, her legs too fat.

She had shocked Aurelio when, early in their honeymoon, she had appeared on the terrace of their Acapulco hotel, standing naked under bushes of bougainvillae and said, "One vagina is like any other."

Their son, Silvio, had been born nine months after this pronouncement and Carlota had turned out to be a devoted mother.

Twenty years into the marriage, disaster had struck in the form of Carlota's diagnosis of pancreatic cancer. Aurelio had consulted specialists from Buenos Aires, Rio and as far away as New York, but the prognosis was grim. "Six months, if she's lucky," the physicians had told them.

Carlota had been philosophical about her fate. "Nothing lasts forever," she had told Aurelio. "It is evident to me that my time on this earth is almost over."

"I'm not giving up," Aurelio had said.

But it was obvious to Carlota that her prospect was grim.

"Nonsense, Aurelio," she had told him, and added, with an odd little laugh, "We will meet again up there, beyond those clouds."

After the death of Carlota, Aurelio had come to the conclusion that the sentimental aspect of his life was over. As lamentable as this omission might be, the thought of pursuing sexual satisfaction seemed an intolerable burden, one which he was willing to forsake.

I'm sixty-five years old, he said to himself. Good

riddance to all that rubbish.

But one day, as he wandered into his office, his secretary announced that an Indian delegation from Ancash was waiting for him in the conference room.

"Good God, Prunella," he said. "Why didn't you get rid of them?"

"They're Indians," Prunella said, scornfully. "I dare anyone to snub them."

"What do they want?"

"Money to build a school."

"My money?"

"If not yours, then King Solomon's."

Aurelio had walked into the conference room looking at his watch and saying, "I have two minutes to hear what you have to say."

When he looked up, what he saw took his breath away.

The Indian delegation consisted of three people. Two men, their skin the colour of bronze and their hair and eyes blacker than coal. The third person was a beautiful young woman. She was white, with long blond hair and eyes the colour of sapphires.

"You are an Indian?" he asked, astonished.

"Yes," she said. "My name is Yupanqui."

He handed the delegation a cheque so enormous they made him Honorary Chairman of the school that would be built some day. Two weeks later he asked Miss Yupanqui, whose name was Coral, to marry him.

"Why?" she asked.

"Because I'm in love with you," he answered.

She seemed perplexed and said she would think about it. A thrill passed through Aurelio. She hadn't turned him down. He waited in silence for her answer to be delivered.

"Think she'll marry me?" he asked Prunella.

"Why wouldn't she?" she said.

"Because she's young and beautiful."

"And you're old and rich. Strikes me as a fair exchange."

Prunella's assumption proved correct. Yes, Coral would marry him. Her only request was that her parents visit every Christmas.

"Of course," he said. "They can stay at the guest cottage in the woods."

The brief ceremony at the Cathedral was attended by the bride and groom, the Yupanquis, Aurelio's son, Silvio and his new wife, Pandora.

"Disgusting, at his age," Pandora said.

"Can't say I blame him," he answered. "She's very beautiful."

"Your mother would not be pleased."

"You can see that he's crazy about her."

"Can't see anything except an old man making a fool of himself."

Aurelio had chosen Rio de Janeiro for their honeymoon, and Coral seemed a bit startled by the sprawling chaotic bustle of the city.

"Like it?" he asked her.

"Well, it is... big," she answered.

He had been surprised that she was a virgin, and rather unaware of the ways of the flesh. It was a strange turn of events, one that depicted her as virtuous – whether her virtue was an illusion or her way of coping with her new husband's animalistic demands.

Patience, he thought, would be its own reward. Such a woman was worth pursuing without a selfish need to force himself on her.

After that first night things were different between them.

Aurelio showed himself a kind and considerate husband. Coral seemed to disguise whatever apprehension she must feel. It seemed to him that her body moved painfully under his efforts. He thought he spied a few tears in her eyes.

"Am I hurting you?"

"No. Of course not."

He paid her compliments and bought her jewels and asked her many times if she was happy. She said she was. When at last the honeymoon ended, he asked her if she would like to stay longer in Rio.

She smiled, then shook her head.

"I'm ready to go home," she said.

FIVE

Coral as a Puzzle

Time was neither friend nor foe, Aurelio Fernandez-Concha thought as he stood in front of the mirror, getting dressed for dinner. He wished he could discover what others saw when they looked at him. An older man, that much was certain. White hair and a carefully trimmed white beard. But the eyes were youthful and his body was still strong.

He wondered what his late wife, Carlota, who used to call him "my Adonis" might say today. He suspected she might sneer, Come, come, no use pretending you're younger than you are, even if you're prancing around with a Lolita on your arm.

He chose an elegant red tie with grey seashells. Peering over his shoulder, he saw that Coral, his wife of three years, was wearing a stunning blue dress, but seemed uncertain about her choice of ear-rings.

"Why not your sapphires?" he said.

"To impress that boring little fellow?" she retorted.

"I thought you liked Professor Greene."

"What is there to like about him? Bald. Loud. A heavy smoker. And inquisitive as hell. Always asking questions and mulling over the answers."

"He seems to have known your parents."

"Assuming the Harringtons *were* my parents."

"Weren't they?"

"I suppose so. If they weren't, who was?"

"Well," Aurelio said with a chuckle. "I'm pleased to announce that Professor Greene is not coming alone. He's bringing a friend with him."

There was a pause during which Coral rejected the sapphires in favour of simple gold clips.

"Who is the friend?" she asked.

"A fellow named Stefan Larsen, an English journalist," he answered.

"A snoop."

"A snoop?"

"All journalists are snoops. How do you think we get all that rubbish in the newspapers?"

"This fellow is doing a piece on San Marcos University."

"Heaven help them. He will probably distort the facts and ruin their reputation."

"Why would he do that?"

"Because newspapers wouldn't sell without a touch of scandal."

"I beg to differ," Aurelio said, and added after a pause, "but let's not quarrel. They won't stay long. One quick drink and I'll make it obvious they must go."

Coral walked over to the mirror and put her arms around her husband. "You're the only person with whom I never want to quarrel," she said.

Cocktails were being served on the verandah, which boasted Aurelio's fondness for orchids. Dozens of them, all sizes, all species, all colours.

"They are as close to perfection as the Good Lord ever created... except when He made you, my dear," Aurelio said.

"You are always kind," she answered.

As they entered the verandah, they realised their erroneous impression of the English journalist, at least where his physical appearance was concerned. Tall, well built, with muscular shoulders and a handsome face – green eyes that seemed curious yet respectful. He was dressed in jeans and an open white shirt, in contrast to the professor who was wearing a brown suit and a brown tie.

"Sit down, sit down," Aurelio said, as if he had been caught in a situation that was rather unexpected.

The butler, a tall Chinese fellow named Xi, came to the portico carrying a tray with three flutes of pink champagne and a glass of whisky.

"I'm a whisky guy," Aurelio explained, "but my wife loves champagne. Hope you do, too."

They toasted each other's health, "*Salud, salud,*" and nibbled on bits of toast topped with caviar, and talked about the mist that was descending on the garden.

"It's called *neblina*," Aurelio told them. "I'm afraid it's as much a part of our city as sunshine."

Then the English journalist, named Stefan, broke into the conversation.

"I'm sorry to disrupt the beauty of this misty afternoon," he said. "But I'm here for a reason, which may be rather startling, coming from a stranger."

"It won't be a surprise," Aurelio told him. "Professor Greene has already mentioned the Harringtons."

"They were my parents' best friends," Stefan explained, "which is the reason why they asked me to pursue this matter."

When Coral spoke, everyone turned to her with

a mixture of apprehension and curiosity. "Go ahead," she said. "Tell us what your parents want to know."

His eyes paused on her face for the first time since they had met. His voice would have been blunt, had it not been so quiet. "They want to know if you are the child who was rescued from the avalanche. If you are, it's almost certain the Harringtons were your parents."

"Nothing is certain in this world," Aurelio said, sipping his whisky. "There is a question of probability. But we cannot establish absolute proof."

"I'm afraid I disagree," Stefan said. "If the probability is overwhelming, chances are the matter is settled."

"I was saved from the mudslide by an Indian named Yupanqui," Coral said. "He and his wife raised me. They're the only parents I've ever known."

That was all there was: the rescue from the mudslide – a triumphant moment that changed a life forever.

"God bless them for their kind deed," Professor Greene said, lighting his second Marlboro. "But they're not your parents. The Harringtons are."

There was a pause during which Professor Greene seemed to consider what he was about to say. "There is no proof of DNA," he added, flicking ashes into a silver ashtray. "But it is an absolute certainty that Keith and Margo Harrington were your parents."

Bestowing first names on them seemed to bring the Harringtons into the verandah; they were no longer ghosts but flesh and blood, proof that the events being discussed had indeed taken place.

The silence seemed cluttered by memories which appeared too far-fetched and morbid to be real. And yet –

"I don't mean to be rude," Aurelio said, sounding uncomfortable, "but we're expected at a dinner some twenty minutes away. We'll have to drive slowly in this fog."

His guests got up at once. Aurelio and his wife did, too. They walked with them through the garden and all the way to the front door.

"We hope you will come back," Coral said, and took her husband's arm.

With her long hair and lovely face, she could have stepped out of a Renoir painting.

SIX

Mischief as a Tool

Except for Coral's husband and her English friends, everyone pronounced her name with the accent on the second syllable. She had attempted to correct them, but had come to the conclusion that her name, however it might be pronounced, was of no consequence to anyone except herself.

"A matter of no importance," she thought.

She was in the garden, cutting long-stemmed red roses and placing them in a basket. Lifting her head, she saw Silvio's heavily pregnant wife waddling towards her.

"Hello, Pandora," Coral said. "How do you like the roses?"

"Wilted and drooping, aren't they?" Pandora said, wiping drops of perspiration off her face with an elegant lace handkerchief.

There was a silence during which Coral was reminded that Pandora had put the fear of God into her when discovering that Coral did not attend Mass, did not confess, and did not take Communion every Sunday.

"You'll burn in Hell," Pandora had told her.

"Me?"

"Yes. You. Your behaviour is a disgrace."

Now standing in the garden, Pandora blurted out in an irritated voice. "I must ask you to fire that maid."

"What maid?"

"Yours."

"You mean Josefa? Why?"

"The woman is a whore. She's after Silvio."

"What makes you think so?"

"Silvio told me. He said she pounced on him while I was visiting my mother."

Coral looked away. She could not bring herself to tell Silvio's wife what she knew.

"I'm not sure you're aware of the facts," she said.

"What facts?"

"Who did what to whom."

"What are you implying?"

Coral did not answer the question. She waited a few moments.

"If you want my advice," she said, angrily, "I would forget the whole thing."

"Well, don't bite my head off."

Coral cut a long-stemmed red rose and a thorn pricked her finger. "Damn," she said, and went on, "Josefa is an excellent maid. I don't want to let her go."

"How can you be so rude? What about me?"

"I'll make sure she's not in your way... or Silvio's."

"Not good enough. I want that whore out of this house."

"It's my house, too, Pandora."

"Then I'm forced to take the matter up with Aurelio."

"If you must, you must."

Aurelio brought up the subject as he and Coral were dressing for dinner. He was examining his collection of neckties, unable to decide.

"Green or blue?" he asked his wife, who was looking in the mirror, applying a new shade of mauve lipstick.

"Red," she said, "the one with grey seashells."

"Again?"

"Why not? It's my favourite."

"Red it is," he said and added, after a pause, "There is something I meant to tell you."

"What is it?" she asked.

"Something rather disagreeable."

"Oh, dear."

"Blackmail, that's what it is. There's no other word for it."

"You're talking about Pandora."

"She told me that if it's a boy, they'll name him Aurelio, after me. She kept displaying that big bump of hers while raging against Josefa."

Was there a veiled repproach in his voice? Did he wish it might be Coral's bump instead of the other woman's?

"Aurelio," Coral said. "Josefa is innocent of any wrongdoing. If anyone is at fault, it's Silvio, not her."

"Well, he does like the ladies," Aurelio agreed. "The question is, will Pandora have a fit if we don't fire the maid."

"I'm not getting rid of Josefa."

"I dare say, that settles the matter. I will tell her you absolutely refused."

Pandora was hystrical at the dinner table, but Aurelio kept calm. "When you have time to reflect, it will not seem so important," he said.

"And what do you expect me to do when that woman throws herself at my husband?"

"Silvio can defend himself, can't you, old boy?"

"Depends," Silvio grinned, "who I'm defending

myself against."

"That whore," his wife sniffled. "Who else?"

"I suppose we can keep our bedroom door locked," Silvio suggested.

"If she's madly in love with you, that won't keep her away," his wife said.

"Love has got nothing to do with it," Aurelio concluded, and he signaled Xi to serve the roast.

SEVEN

Blue Skies, Green Trees and Silvio

She galloped with a thrilling sense of adventure, leaving the mansion behind, and heading towards the hills that would lead to a long road all the way to the next town, named Cochabamba, which boasted field after field of soft white cotton as far as the eye could see.

"Cotton, Monsieur Brown," she shouted to him. "Precious stuff, isn't it?"

The horse flattened his ears and turned back his head as if something had caught his attention. A few moments later Coral found herself galloping next to the English journalist, who was riding Aurelio's mare, Mona Lisa.

"Red soil, green hills and a beautiful young woman galloping next to me," he smiled. "Whoever said that life isn't perfect?"

"You're riding Mona Lisa," Coral replied. "How did that happen?"

"Thanks to Mr. Fernandez-Concha. I've never known a more generous host."

"You can call him Aurelio. Everyone does." A pause. "You can call me Coral."

"Stefan," he said.

Tall spindly poplars flew past as they rode across the fields towards a path that boasted an arrow pointing east.

"Where are we going?" he asked.

"A town named Cochabamba. Quite picturesque. You'll like it."

The horses galloped as though they knew the way through the deserted road. A few minutes later, they entered the town – cobblestone streets, mud huts built with adobe rather than brick, a market place and a tiny church among banana trees, sunflowers and strawberry fields.

"Here we are," Coral said, as they dismounted and tied up their horses.

"Would you like a coffee?" he asked.

"There is a tavern nearby called *Cielito Lindo*. We can get a coffee for ourselves and water for the horses."

As they approached the tavern Coral saw Silvio's black Cherokee jeep parked on the other side of the street.

Damn, she thought, but it was too late to turn back. They went in.

Silvio was sitting at a table, drinking a beer and smoking a cigarette.

Though she disliked him, Coral could understand what people who found him attractive saw in him. A swarthy face with thick lips that were always sneering. Big shoulders, a muscular chest. The word one associated with him was *dark* – dark hair, dark eyes and a rather dark disposition that just escaped being nasty.

He got up and bowed with exaggerated courtesy as Coral and the English journalist came in.

"Have you been breaking any hearts today?" he asked her, with a grin.

She gave him a chilly stare and said, "Silvio, this is Stefan Larsen." And to Stefan, "This is Aurelio's son, Silvio."

The two men shook hands. Silvio went back to his beer, while Coral and Stefan settled at the counter and ordered coffee.

"Another beer," Silvio shouted.

A pretty, dark-skinned waitress served him.

"What's your name, sweetheart?" Silvio asked.

"Rosita, *señor*."

"Come sit on my lap, Rosita."

"I can't, *señor.* I have to serve the customers."

Silvio reached out and pulled the waitress onto his lap.

"Let's do a lap dance," he said with a grin.

But the girl looked frightened and was making an effort to free herself.

The owner of the tavern, an older man with white whiskers named Mr. Perez, approached Silvio.

"Please let her go, *señor.* She has to serve the customers."

"Get lost," Silvio said, and pushed him away with his foot.

Stefan rose from the counter and walked over to Silvio.

"Let the girl go," he said, in a calm voice.

"Who asked for your opinion?" Silvio responded.

"Let her go."

Either the icy calm in Stefan's voice, or the hidden threat he might detect, prompted Silvio to release his grip. The girl scampered away and hid behind the counter next to the owner.

Silvio stood up and punched Stefan in the stomach.

"Fuck off," he said.

Stefan slammed his fist into Silvio's face so hard, he staggered backwards and crashed against the wall. He raised his hand to his cheek and, to punish him, he went over to Coral and said, "Is this the asshole with whom you're betraying my father?"

Lifting her head, Coral saw the rage in his eyes, and a sense of fear invaded her. Fear, plain and simple, with its obvious threat and implications.

"Please go, Silvio," she said.

Silvio addressed Stefan one more time.

"You'll be sorry for this," he said, and left.

Through the open door, they could hear the jeep's engine as it roared away.

Stefan went back to the counter and sat next to Coral.

"Sorry you had to be exposed to this unpleasant incident," he said.

"No surprise to me," Coral answered.

Both Mr. Perez and Rosita held out their hand to shake Stefan's.

"Thank you, *señor*," they said.

Coral felt a little lump in her throat. She reflected that such a thing as kindness was a far more exhausting emotion than rage.

To her surprise, Stefan placed his hand on her arm. "Believe me," he told her. "Not worth thinking about."

EIGHT

Of Love and Happiness

Josefa's boyfriend, Rocco, was a tall strong Indian who worshipped the ground she walked on. He was also a devout Catholic who never missed Mass at the tiny church of the *Señor de los Milagros*, in Cochabamba.

"You won't believe what Father Severino told me yesterday," he said, looking upset.

"What did he tell you?" Josefa asked.

"He said you and I are living in sin."

It occured to Josefa that "sin" was a tricky word, one that no two people could easily agree on.

"We love each other," she said. "Isn't that enough?"

"Father Severino doesn't think so."

"What did he say?"

"He said our children would be bastards."

"But we don't have any."

"When we do, they will be bastards. He also said that when we die, we will go to Hell."

"We're young," Josefa told him. "Neither one of us is sick. I don't think we're in danger of dying."

Rocco took her hand and raised it to his lips. His thick black hair covered his face, the colour of bronze, and his voice had the tenderness that thrilled his soul whenever he spoke to her.

"Josefa," he said. "I think we should marry."

When Josefa made the suggestion to Coral, she responded with great joy. "Brilliant idea," she said. "I will be your matron of honour and will order your gown. White satin with little pearls embroidered on the front, all the way down to the waist."

"Will *señor* Aurelio be our *padrino*?" Josefa asked.

"I'm sure he will," Coral told her.

But Aurelio, somewhat bewildered, declined. "I'm too old," he said. "They need a young person who can look after their children for many years to come."

Coral was afraid he might suggest his son, Silvio, but, mercifully, he did not.

"Why don't you ask Stefan Larsen, the English journalist," he said. "As a gentleman, I can always tell if another man is a gentleman."

"You think he is?"

"Yes," Aurelio concluded. "Something about him suggests good breeding."

The wedding day dawned brilliant and beautiful. Not a cloud in the sky, a soft breeze stirring the poplars, and, as they approached the church, a smell of jasmine in the air.

Josefa looked pretty in her wedding gown and Rocco was at his best in white pants and a white *guayabera*. Coral had chosen a stunning dress, sapphire blue, and Stefan wore a grey suit and a blue tie.

Father Severino, who suffered from a highly emphatic oratory, took advantage of the occasion to deliver what he considered an inspired sermon. "Servants of God," he called the congregation of twelve people, and went on to quote the Spanish playright, Calderón de la Barca. "For the two of you, *la vida es sueño*", he said and translated for the benefit of anyone who didn't understand, Life is a dream.

As they left the church and headed to Rocco's cabin in the woods, where a wedding lunch had been arranged, an unpleasant incident took place. Silvio's heavily pregnant wife, Pandora, emerged from the black jeep, waddled towards Josefa and spat on her face.

"Whore," she said.

Then she climbed back into the jeep and sped away.

Coral felt a spasm of fury she was barely able to control. She wiped Josefa's face with her handkerchief and kissed her.

"Don't mind her," she said. "She's a very unhappy woman."

The cabin had been decorated with garlands of white roses and the luncheon table boasted white rose petals and elegant china which Coral had provided. Aurelio had sent a magnificent wedding cake, and Stefan had ordered a case of Laurent Perrier and two cases of Pinot Noir.

The food was delicious, *ceviche* to start, followed by *lomito saltado* (stir-fried beef) with rice. Half-way through lunch, a band of musicians who called themselves *Los Bandoleros* played their favourite music and everyone waited until Stefan took Josefa to the dance floor, followed by Rocco and Coral. After twirling a few times, Rocco danced with Josefa and Coral found herself in Stefan's arms.

In the complicated realm of human emotions, Coral wondered if the so-called "physical attraction" might be immensely more complicated and less easily understood. What am I feeling? What is this sense of dizziness that has come over me? Idle, ornamental people such as herself, accepted them indifferently, if they recognised them at all. There might even be a disoriented detachment, a mixture of aloofness and loss which afflicted women who regarded themselves as disdainful of passion.

"My head is in a twirl," she told Stefan, as they moved faster on the dance floor. "I'm afraid I may fall."

"You won't," he told her, and tightened his hold around her. "While you're in my arms, you will never fall."

The band was now playing *The Bride Cuts the Cake* and Stefan, his arm firmly holding Coral's waist, led her to the table.

Leaning against him, she placed a spoonful of cake in her mouth. Sweet. So sweet. If one had always savoured sugar and spice, there might be times when nothing else would taste the way it should.

NINE

An Ounce of Common Sense

Pandora's mother, Yolanda, was a large woman in more ways than one. Large hips, large breasts, big hair piled up into a honeycomb with a few wisps escaping onto her temples.

She was also "large" in her attitude to others. *Largesse oblige*, she was fond of saying. Until someone pointed out that she probably meant, *Noblesse oblige*. Nonsense, Yolanda retorted. I said *largesse* and I meant *largesse*.

Her husband, Anselmo, has disgraced the family by falling in love with his Mexican secretary and moving to Guadalajara. Yolanda had divorced him *in absentia* and never mentioned him again. A few postcards arrived from Mexico, addressed to Pandora, who destroyed them without reading them.

When Pandora started dating Silvio Fernandez-Concha, her mother said, "You would do well to marry him. His family is wealthy and powerful."

"Doubt he wants to get married," Pandora said.

"If you play your cards right, he will."

"How do I do that?"

"Give him everything he wants, except sex."

The formula worked and the nuptials of Silvio and Pandora became the wedding of the year.

Now, the forthcoming arrival of her first grandchild gave Yolanda an agreeable sense of security, which was rattled by Pandora, who said, "Mummy, Silvio is interested in other women. He may be having an affair."

Yolanda, who regarded jealousy as unhealthy, came to the rescue. "What do you care?" she said. "You're the wife. The others are only the *queridas*."

As she arrived at Aurelio's for a cocktail before dinner, Yolanda was startled to see Silvio's red, swollen cheek.

"What happened to your face?" she asked.

"I was playing polo," he said. "I took a spill."

"You might consider changing sports," Yolanda said. "Ping-pong might be a better choice."

She found Aurelio at the verandah, with that blond wisp of a girl he had married, the daughter of Indians from the Sierra. Trash. How the devil did she ever get him? Sex, no doubt. Men were such pigs. He probably flattered himself on his perception of romance. Women loved *him*, not his money.

Aurelio rose at once and kissed Yolanda on both cheeks. Coral smiled pleasantly and offered her a glass of champagne.

"Don't care for it," Yolanda said. "I'll have a whisky... But don't call that Chinese fellow. I don't care for him either."

"I'll get it," Aurelio said, and left the verandah.

"Any bun in the oven yet?" Yolanda asked Coral, when they were alone.

"Not yet," Coral said.

"I would hurry, if I were you. For Aurelio's sake. At his age, it's unlikely he will go on forever."

"He's strong and in good health."

"You're not obliged to follow my advice, but I would get pregnant if I were you. If you had an ounce of common sense, you would realise it's the only way to satisfy Aurelio's vanity."

"I'm more interested in his happiness."

"Where men are concerned, vanity and happiness are one and the same."

Aurelio returned with a glass of whisky for Yolanda.

"What have I missed?" he asked. "What was it you said about happiness?"

"We were talking about the blue bird of happiness," Coral smiled.

"Never heard of it," Yolanda said.

"The blue bird of happiness is in your own back yard," Coral told her.

"Nonsense," Yolanda retorted. "If that is what you think, you won't care a packet of pins whether you ever find what you're looking for."

Aurelio smiled and put an arm around his wife. "I've found it," he said.

TEN

San Marcos University

Stefan Larsen's essay on San Marcos University was thoroughly researched, expertly presented and a bit tongue-in-cheek.

"If Shakespeare had attended San Marcos University, Hamlet would have a happy ending," he had written.

The essay had been published in the editorial page of The New York Times, which seemed interested in the fact that the university had started at the time of the Viceroys, on May 1551, in the chamber of the Rosario Convent, of the Dominican order.

In addition, the article had been picked up by The Daily Telegraph and the Daily Mail, in London, as well as two Peruvian newspapers, *El Comercio* and *La Prensa*. Though they had published the quotation, *Adelante tu Siempre Estarás*, they had sneered at the fact that the essay had been written by an English journalist. What the hell was the matter with the Peruvian press? Was there no one who could have taken on this task?

Professor Greene had telephoned Stefan at his hotel, *Los Laureles*, in Miraflores, and invited himself to breakfast.

He arrived in his trademark brown suit and brown tie and found Stefan sitting in the garden, under a white umbrella, dressed in jeans and a white T-shirt.

"Here is the breakfast menu," he said to the professor, after shaking hands. "I suggest we order. It gets very crowded at this time."

Professor Greene ordered a ham omelette, toast and *café con leche*. Stefan did not depart from his usual black coffee and croissants.

"Well done, my boy," Professor Greene said. "I learned something I didn't know."

"What was that?"

"The fact the university was chartered by a royal decree, signed by Charles V, Holy Roman Emperor."

"Well, you know, I imagine anyone could have written the essay. You don't need a fertile imagination. Just facts."

The professor opened his mouth, but the words

seemed reluctant to come out.

"Since your work is done," he said, at last, "I expect you will soon go back to London."

"I haven't made any plans," Stefan answered.

Their food arrived, and the professor ate a few mouthfuls before he spoke.

"The reason I mention it is that I received an e-mail from your father and a letter from your mother."

"Is that so? What about?"

There was a sense of embarrassment in the professor's silence. He did not seem eager to respond and the prolonged pause prompted Stefan to repeat the question.

"What about?" he asked.

"The rumours," the professor said.

"What rumours?"

"About you and Mrs. Fernandez-Concha."

Stefan frowned. The words seemed to float awkwardly in the air, creating a greater sense of discomfort than he had expected. He had never given a thought to such things as reasons, or excuses. Telling a lie was another story.

"I have a great regard for both Mr. and Mrs. Fernandez-Concha," he said.

"I don't doubt it," the professor replied.

"I'm sure you wouldn't tell me anything that isn't

common knowledge. The problem seems to be with the way a situation is perceived."

"That's correct."

"What may be an innocent occurrence to some, may appear infamous to others."

"Quite," the professor said, looking unconvinced.

"What I do is nobody's business, except my own."

"Whether that is true or not, what comes to mind is a Chinese proverb."

"Perhaps you will tell me what it is."

"Steal a whole country and they make you prince. Steal a fish hook and they hang you."

Stefan laughed. "I don't supose you're suggesting I may hang for whatever pecadillo I may have committed."

"Our society doesn't hang people for trivial offences."

"Point taken," Stefan concluded, and he asked the waiter for the bill.

ELEVEN

An Afternoon to Remember

They were unable to go riding in the morning because Coral had to meet with the ladies of the Garden Club.

"What are they like?" Stefan had asked.

"Roses and thorns," she had told him. "But mostly thorns."

So they started in the early afternoon, which proved to be a good decision. There was not a cloud in the sky and the air was cool and fresh after the morning drizzle.

Riding next to her, Stefan reflected that this pattern of closeness and distance had repeated itself for almost three weeks, while London receded into the distance, Parliament voted not to strike Syria, the Americans prepared to do the opposite, a building collapsed in Bangladesh killing dozens, a 6.5 magnitude earthquake struck eastern China and bulls ran on the streets of Seville enthralling the crowds.

Do I dare approach her? he wondered, and concluded that it might be as ungallant to do so as it would be not to. The question lingered in his mind, unanswered. There seemed to be a mysterious weakness within himself which he could neither understand nor reverse. I believe in reason, he thought, but, in the absence of reason, what do I believe in?

Halfway to Cochabamba, Coral slowed down and eventually stopped. Stefan turned his horse and trotted back to her.

"Enough?" he asked her. "Would you rather go back?"

"You mind?"

"Not at all."

They cantered back to the plantation and headed for the barn where they dismounted, removed their saddles and bridles and led the horses into their stalls.

As he prepared to follow her to the main house, he saw that she had turned south towards a path that led across the lawn to a clearing in the woods. A cottage stood nearby, among poplars and olive trees. It boasted its own garden, orchard and fountain.

Coral took out a key and inserted it into the lock. Her face was hushed, her eyes downcast. The door opened with a creak.

"I've never done this before," she said.

They walked into a brightly furnished living room with plush carpets, paintings and a bunch of roses in a bowl. Coral closed the door and locked it.

He took her in his arms and lowered her down onto the plush carpet, there, just inside the locked door.

"I want you," he told her. "I've never wanted a woman so much."

"I want you, too," she said.

Their lovemaking was smooth, yet furious, knees between thighs, whispers disconcertingly bold, and sensation, only sensation, demanding, tantalising, and strong. Too strong. It consumed itself almost at once.

"The bedroom is over there," Coral said, and staggered to her feet.

He rose and swept her up. The bed was in an alcove, discreet, enormous, with huge pillows and embroidered sheets.

Again, he said, "I want you."

And she answered, "So do I."

He looked with awe upon the beauty of her body as they took off their clothes, shirts, pants, a slip, soft underwear, thin, transparent, and her thighs, open to him, her voice almost anguished as she murmured words she had never uttered before, yet breathless in their sincerity, Yes, touch me, and he, too, sinking into a landscape he had known existed but never explored, not like this, not in the way he found himself, dizzyingly, stumbling on the edge of ecstasy.

The intensity of their orgasm left them stunned, shaken and yet profoundly at peace.

"My life will never be the same again," he told her.

"Nor mine," she said.

Afterwards, they fell asleep.

Coral opened her eyes to a red sky outside the window. The sun was going down beyond the hills.

"Stefan," she said, her voice blurred by sleep. "It's getting late. I've got to go home."

He got up at once. Then, without a word, they got dressed and made the bed. Coral took the key and locked the door. It seemed absurd that they should part, and yet, he watched her turn north towards the path that led to the main house.

She waved to him without turning, and it seemed to Stefan that this gesture would be unforgettable, perhaps the most vivid of all his memories.

He waited until she disappeared behind the hedges. For a moment he stood there, not knowing if he should follow her. And if he did, what then? The gnawing doubt subsided, to be replaced by common sense.

Don't be a fool, he thought. Happiness is frail. How does anyone know whether it will endure. Or whether it will come and go. Quickly. Like a bolt of lightning.

He got into his car which was parked behind the barn and drove to his hotel.

TWELVE

A Tavern called *Cielito Lindo*

Two days later, they galloped to Cochabamba, tied up their horses and went into their favourite tavern, *Cielito Lindo*, for a coffee. At that time of the morning, they were the only customers.

Both the owner, Mr. Perez, and Rosita were delighted to see them.

"We have bread pudding," Rosita said and served two slices with their coffee.

"Delicious," Coral said.

"Another slice?" Stefan asked.

They left the counter and settled in a small alcove with their coffee.

Then, strangely, Stefan asked a question which was as disconcerting as it was unexpected.

"You remember the mudslide?" he said.

She looked at him and reflected that his concern

was obviously a desire to lighten the burden of her memory rather than satisfy an idle curiosity.

"Yes," she said. "I do."

"What do you remember most?"

"Letting go of my father's hand and watching him disappear under the mud. My mother was already lost. And then – "

"What then?"

"I was dragged by the current, faster and faster towards the mud."

"You went under?"

"No. I continued to float. That was when I saw that a huge Indian was throwing himself into the mud in order to rescue me."

"Mr. Yupanqui."

"Yes. He grabbed my arm and kept me afloat while making a desperate effort to reach the bank of the river onto a marsh that was not covered by mud."

"What were you thinking?"

"I don't remember. The concept of death must have escaped my perception."

"How old were you?"

"Six. Old enough to remember but not to understand that loss is irreparable."

He raised her hand and touched his lips to her wrist.

"What happend when Mr. Yupanqui reached the bank of the river? he asked.

"He saw that I was crying, desperately wanting to find my parents. He seemed to understand and spoke to me in a language I had never heard."

"*Quechua*?"

"Yes."

"And then?"

"Other Indians came running out of their cabins, his wife among them. She picked me up and held me in her arms."

She frowned at the memory and remained silent.

"I'd like to meet them," Stefan said.

"You will. They speak only *Quechua*, but I can translate."

"Strange, isn't it? So long ago and you haven't forgotten."

Stefan paid, and they said goodbye to Mr. Perez and Rosita, then galloped all the way back.

"I can never leave you without pain," Coral said, as they led the horses into the barn.

"You're not leaving me," Stefan told her. "You're with me even when you're not."

"Tomorrow, then?"

"Yes. But I want you to think."

"About what?"

"Us. Aurelio. What we're going to do."

"I can't think."

"You have to."

"I'll try, but I feel…"

"What?"

"Frail… like an autumn leaf about to be blown away."

"You won't be, I promise."

"Goodbye," Coral said.

But she did not let go of him. She held on, tightly, as if she did not care if she made herself ridiculous.

On Stefan's brow was an uneasy frown, and yet he smiled at her.

"Until tomorrow," he said.

THIRTEEN

Gossip and Mischief

Pandora gave birth to a baby girl they named Yolanda, after Pandora's mother. Going upstairs into the Maternity Wing, Aurelio ran into his son, Silvio, who was leaving the hospital.

"We'll keep trying until we get a boy, and we'll name him after you." Silvio said.

Aurelio laid down the enormous bouquet of pink roses so he could embrace his son.

"Very happy with my grandchild," he said. "Boy or girl."

He reclaimed his flowers and was about to continue up the stairs, but Silvio's voice stopped him.

"Father," he said. "I am most dreadfully sorry about the rumours."

"What rumours?"

"You haven't heard?"

"No."

Silvio hesitated. "Maybe I shouldn't meddle," he said. "If the rumours are true, they'll find their way to you."

Aurelio's voice showed an astounding irritation. "Silvio," he said. "I detest gossip, whether true or false. What the hell are you talking about?"

"Your wife," he said. "She's supposed to be having an affair with the English journalist."

"You have heard this?"

"Yes."

"From whom?"

"Everyone I've talked to."

"I don't believe it."

"Suit yourself. As they say, the husband is the last to know."

This time Silvio rushed downstairs, leaving his father with his agitated look, his chagrin and his roses.

Aurelio found his wife fast asleep on a chaise-longue near the pool. He leaned over and gently stirred her awake. His heart was dreadfully heavy as she looked up and smiled at him.

"I just came from seeing Pandora," Aurelio said.

"How nice. I'll go this afternoon."

"I ran into Silvio as I was coming in."

"Oh? Did he seem happy?"

"Not exactly."

"I don't see it's Pandora's fault... having a girl, I mean."

Aurelio reflected for a moment. He wished he did not have to bring up this unpleasant subject. He supposed that the possibility of his wife being unfaithful was remote, but it had to be pursued.

"You may find this awkward," he said. "But the source of Silvio's displeasure is not Pandora. It's you."

She sat up in the chair, looking puzzled. Aurelio did not speak for a moment, then he said, "He thinks you're having an affair with Stefan Larsen."

Coral sat back. She no longer looked startled, only amused. The beginning of a smile raised the corner of her lips.

"Is that all?" she said.

He was taken aback by her reaction.

"You mean you're not?" he asked, in a voice that begged for reassurance.

"Of course not," Coral said, and looked at him straight in the face. "That's just Silvio being Silvio."

A sense of relief appeared on Aurelio's face. "Thank Heaven," he said. "I couldn't bear it if what I heard was true."

The next afternoon, as she prepared to meet

Stefan at his hotel, she wore a large hat, dark glasses and avoided the lift, walking up the back stairs instead.

He took her in his arms the moment she walked in.

"Wait," she said. "There is something I need to tell you."

"It's just as well," he said, when he had heard that Aurelio had fallen prey to Silvio's machinations. "We can't continue like this indefinitely."

"I can't do this to him, Stefan. It's too cruel."

"He's very fair. I think he would understand."

"It would destroy him. It would be like putting his head in a noose."

"So what's the alternative?"

"Waiting."

"How long?"

"I don't know."

Stefan got up and strolled slowly to the window. "I can't stay here much longer," he said. "I have to get back to London. I want you to come with me."

She stood in front of the mirror and gave him a long stare, sadly, almost despairingly.

"I'm at a standstill," she said. "I can't go. And I can't stay."

Their lovemaking was more intense than before, if such a thing was possible. Why it happened and how it had come into existence was as inexplicable as the sun rising, or the rain falling. Some day they might understand why sexual fascination became love. Or, was it the other way around?

"I can't live without you," she said.

"That's good," he answered, "because I can't live without you."

FOURTEEN

A Penny for his Thoughts

Stefan kept insisting he wanted to meet Coral's Indian parents, the Yupanquis.

"But they live in Ancash," she said.

"Where is that?"

"A province in the north of Perú."

"How far away?"

"About an hour flight."

"We can do it. We can charter a plane, go over in the morning, have lunch with them and be back by late afternoon.

So they did.

Coral left word with Josefa that she was attending a meeting at the Garden Club, followed by tea. Should Aurelio wonder if she was expected for dinner, the answer was yes.

Flying over the Andes, Stefan remembered,

from reading world history, the sad tale of the Inca emperor Atahualpa, who had filled a room with gold and silver as ransom to secure his release from prison. The measure had been futile, as the Spanish conquerors had taken the precious metals and killed him anyway.

The Yupanquis looked like Atahualpa. Bronze skin, black hair, muscular arms, a hook nose and eyes like those of an eagle.

"Tell them how pleased I am to meet them," Stefan said.

Coral translated, then said. "They thank you for the sentiment."

If they asked any questions about Aurelio, Coral did not translate them.

"Tell them I'm in love with you," he said. "I have never been so in love before."

Their next question was addressed to Coral. Did she love him in return?

"Yes," she said. "I do."

Despite this assurance, the Yupanquis seemed somewhat skeptical. Their eyes were fixed watchfully on Stefan, and it was possible they held a glimmer of doubt.

"They want to know if we're going to get married," Coral said.

"Tell them yes, as soon as you can get a divorce."

"I won't say that. I'll just say that we hope good things will happen."

"Sounds a bit euphemistic," Stefan said. "But you know best."

The Yupanquis had one last question before serving lunch.

"What is it?"

"A penny for your thoughts," Coral said.

"This is strange," Stefan told them. "I haven't been aware of any thoughts crossing my mind. Until now." He reflected a moment, then added, "To tell you the truth, I'm beginning to think that love is like the sun. We cannot touch it, but we exist because of it."

Coral's translation emerged as a shorter version of his speech. Perhaps the Yupanquis might have found his protestations to contain too many frills and not enough substance.

Lunch was announced.

They sat at a wooden table, with wooden chairs that were not very comfortable, despite some cushions that boasted black sequins.

Mrs. Yupanqui permitted herself a smile of satisfaction as the food appeared on the table.

"Tell him I made it myself," she said.

From the jubilant quality of her voice, Stefan had no doubt the food would be delicious.

Tamales, served in banana leaves, and a beverage called *chicha,* which was made from fermented corn. For dessert, they had *turrón de doña Pepa,* a sweet pastry that crumbled in the mouth and tasted like an exotic version of a pale brownie.

"Please thank your parents for their hospitality," Stefan said.

The Yupanquis nodded and said something that made Coral smile.

"What did they say?"

"They are very pleased to have met you," she said.

"The feeling is mutual," he told them.

When the afternoon came to an end and it was time to say goodbye, Stefan learned that a ritual was required to prevent any malevolent forces from doing harm to them.

Such a ritual was the exchange of gifts.

Coral was prepared. She offered them an illustrated book about London.

The Yupanquis gave Stefan a small sculpture made of stone. Smooth and beautiful, it reminded him of an archaelogical treasure, or a museum piece.

"It's a *tumi,*" Coral told him. "Most likely, their most precious possession."

"But I can't take it from them," he protested.

"You must," she said. "They would be heart-broken if you didn't."

He gave the Yupanquis a warm embrace. They said goodbye to their daughter, obviously with sadness. He thought he spied a glimmer of tears in their eyes.

"This was better than I ever expected," he told Coral, as they climbed into the plane.

"Much," she said.

FIFTEEN

Desire and the Oblique

What Coral didn't know was that Silvio had made up his mind to ignore all the danger signals – his father's distress, his wife's jealousy, the sleepless nights which had preceded this crazy impulse, Coral's scorn and whatever consequence might prove indistinguisable from this gnawing need to satisfy his lust.

There is a perverse indifference in the way she ignores me, he thought. But I don't care. Once I'm inside her, my sole object will be pleasure. Whether she can shrug off her reluctance or not is of no importance. I'm suffering. I need release.

He saw his father leave the house and get into his Rolls. He walked upstairs into the master bedroom to find Josefa cleaning the mirror on the dressing table.

"Where is the *señora*?" he asked.

"I don't know, *señor.*"

He looked out of the window and caught a glimpse of Coral in the garden, dropping seeds into the bird feeder.

He rushed downstairs and arrived a little breathless, hunting among the rose bushes, for she was no longer feeding the birds.

"Coral," he called.

She seemed both startled and annoyed to find him in the garden.

"What do you want?" she asked.

"I need to talk to you."

"Haven't you caused enough damage?"

"Damage?"

"You told your father there were rumours about me. He was very upset."

"He should be, assuming the rumours are true."

"I have nothing to say to you, Silvio. What I do with my life is my own affair."

"You're wrong. If you're turning my father into a pathetic cuckold, it's my affair, too."

"Go away. I don't want to discuss it."

One after the other, her words failed to persuade him to let go. Perhaps the opposite. He knew he could not allow her to leave the garden without listening to him.

"Coral," he said. "What you don't understand is that men can't behave in a certain way without the thought of reward or punishment."

"What is this? A lecture of moral ethics? From someone who has no morals?"

"How can I persuade you that I'm not a villain? I'm simply a man tormented by desire."

"Damn it, Silvio! I am your father's wife. Is that fact of no value to you?"

"It's of no value when you're fucking the English journalist. Why pretend to be so prudish?"

"I've heard enough. Go away."

She was haughty and magnificent and completely unprepared for what happened next. He had ripped open her blouse and was kissing her breasts, while pressing himself against her.

"You know you want it," he said. "Your English lover is an ordinary bloke. Stupid, too. He doesn't understand what a whore you are."

The heat of his passion seemed to burn him from within. There were beads of perspiration on his face; a sort of relentless craving took hold of him as he mumbled rambling drunken words and reached down under her skirt.

Coral shook herself free of him and stepped back.

"Get away from me," she screamed.

"Listen, bitch," he said. "I've been very patient. But I won't wait any longer. I'll get what I want, even if I have to rape you."

Her anger rose like thunder, an explosion of its own engendering.

He did not expect that her hand would rise with such fury. But it did. Harsh and quick. Striking him in the face with such force it caused him to stumble back against the rose bushes.

"Now go to your father and complain about me," she said. "This time you have a reason."

When he finally gathered himself and escaped from the absurdity of the situation, she was gone.

SIXTEEN

Looking at the Waves

The following day brought brilliant sunshine and a warm breeze that caressed the palm fronds. The shiny leaves of poplars, maples and pacay trees boasted various shades of green, from lime to avocado to grasshoppers. Birds twittered with a shrill, pungent cry that made one think of magic violins.

"Let's go to the beach," Coral said to Aurelio, but he declined, explaining that he had to prepare for a meeting of the Textile Federation in Buenos Aires.

"When are you going?" she asked.

"Tomorrow or the next day," Aurelio replied.

When she mentioned it to Stefan, he said it was a great idea.

"Let's go to *La Herradura*," he said. "The beach is beautiful and you can swim for miles with just the brilliant sun and the taste of salt..."

"...and a woman racing to keep up with you."

"We are good at whatever we do together," he told her.

He stretched out on the sand after the long swim. She twisted the water out of her hair and lay down beside him. At the end of the pier a little red flag was fluttering in the breeze. He turned over and kissed her shoulder.

"Did you ever think that happiness would be defined as a little red flag?" he asked.

"Only if it flutters," she answered.

They were silent for some time, and when she spoke again, her voice was quiet and the question that rose to her lips seemed awkward and hesitant.

"Stefan," she said. "In all the years of working as a journalist, have you ever come upon the subject of rape?"

He answered without hesitation. "I'm afraid I have," he said. "A young woman in Kabul was raped by two men, but instead of being recognised as a victim, she was found guilty of a "moral crime" and sent to prison. Most dreadfully unfair." He paused a moment, then said, "Why do you ask?"

She spoke with great reluctance about Silvio's aggression in the garden. She was obviously ambivalent about wanting to discuss such unpleasant behaviour.

"It's probably far less important than it seems," she said.

"On the contrary," Stefan told her. "It defines Silvio exactly as he is. The deepest roots of rape, as I have learned from textbooks on the subjhect, seem to deal with a man's cult of masculinity and aggression."

"Aggression. Always aggression. Is that the ultimate definition of a man's behaviour?"

"Not all men. We're talking about Silvio, remember? In his case, his conduct goes beyond sexual conquest and becomes a cultural abnormality."

Coral reflected on these words. Stefan had not jumped to conclusions or analysed a situation quite mechanically. He had simply interpreted the message that her story had conveyed.

"As I understand it," she said, "Silvio has always been a rough character."

"That may be," he said. "We can forgive him those rough edges, but rape was never part of the deal."

"So... what can I expect from him? Love? Hate?"

"Love and hate... in equal measures."

An old woman walked by selling *picarones* with honey. They bought some and ate them with their fingers on a paper plate.

"I shall miss all of it," Stefan said.

"What do you mean?" she asked.

"I'm going back to London day after tomorrow. The Daily Telegraph wants me to cover the Prime Minister's meeting with European dignitaries. If I don't they'll give the assignment to someone else."

Like sound, silence seemed incredibly loud – seagulls, a siren, the waves, the beat of a helicopter, the chug-chug of a fishing boat.

Coral's face was turned away from him. If a word could define it, it would be aloof.

"Which brings me back to us," Stefan said.

"Always does," she said, with a smile. "Whether for style, or substance."

"I'm serious. You are all I care about, Coral."

"That may be, but you're leaving anyway."

"I don't want to leave without you. I have purchased two British Airways tickets from Lima to London. One of them is for you. I hope you will use it. I'm looking forward so much to putting everything behind us and moving on."

He wished she would stop looking at the waves and turn her attention to him. When she did, her face seemed to suggest that she understood what was happening to them.

Stefan had yielded to a situation that was far

from ordinary and they now found themselves faced with an intolerable choice. Damned if I do, damned if I don't.

"Day after tomorrow?" she asked, in a voice that betrayed no anxiety, no distress.

"Yes," he told her.

"Well," she said. "That leaves all of tomorrow, doesn't it?"

SEVENTEEN

When Minutes turn into Hours

Next day a number of things occurred that were somewhat unexpected.

Aurelio left for Buenos Aires a day early to give the introductory remarks to the Textile Federation.

"A dubious honour and a colossal bore," he told his wife.

Pandora packed several suitcases and announced that she and the baby were spending a few days at the Club Esmeralda, in Ancón, with her mother. Silvio promised to join her as soon as he could.

Josefa found Coral getting dressed in the bedroom and said, "I had a bad dream last night."

"What was it?"

"Someone was trying to hurt you."

"Don't worry, Josefa. It was just a dream. No one

is trying to hurt me."

She had arranged to meet Stefan at four o'clock at the cottage and arrived a few minutes late.

"I waited hours," he told her.

"Minutes."

"Without you the minutes turn into hours."

They held each other tightly and said nothing more. The trip to London was not discussed, but her silence spoke volumes.

A moment later they heard a sound they had not expected. Someone had inserted a key in the lock. The door opened with a creak and Silvio came in. He was holding a roll of twine in one hand and a gun in the other. The gun appeared to be a semi-automatic pistol.

"Romeo and Juliet, without the balcony," he said.

"What do you want?" Coral asked him.

"You will soon find out," he said, and threw the roll of twine at her.

She caught it and looked stunned, rather than frightened.

"Tie him to the bedpost," Silvio told her. "Hands behind his back. Facing the bed. I want him to watch what you and I are going to do."

"What makes you think I will?" Coral said.

"You will," Silvio told her, and waved the gun at

Stefan. "He won't look pretty with a bullet between the eyes."

"Don't be afraid," Stefan told Coral. "Just do as he says."

Coral did. She tied Stefan to the bedpost, his hands behind his back.

"Good," Silvio said, and moved towards Coral.

Furiously, she now backed away from him. "Don't touch me," she yelled. "Don't come near me."

"Get away from her," Stefan shouted.

"For God's sake, Coral," Silvio said. "Don't you understand? I've got you in the brain."

He laid his gun down on the night table, then slammed Coral on the bed and threw himself on top of her, ripping open her blouse and kissing her breasts, while his hand explored below.

Coral stiffened beneath him and pushed him away. There was a distinct odour of perspiration emanating from him. Perhaps it was her. Both?

Within himself, Silvio endured an almost convulsive anguish, a need to penetrate that tight small hole and let her feel the grip of his hands on her hips, up and down, up and down, until his throbbing stopped, fulfilled, exhausted.

"Spread your legs, whore," he murmured. "You know you want it."

"Get off me," Coral screamed, as Stefan tried and failed to loosen his bindings.

There was a sudden blast of air as the door burst open and Rocco came in, holding an AK-47 assault rifle. His eyes flashed angrily as he walked over to the bed.

"Get off her," he shouted at Silvio.

Silvio watched him over his shoulder.

"Fuck off, *maricón*," he said, and reached out for his gun.

Rocco slapped the gun off the night table and watched it fall and slide across the floor, all the way to the other end of the room.

Again, he said, "Get off her."

Silvio's face was flushed. Rage had made him sweat. There were beads of perspiration on his forehead. He gathered whatever leftover arrogance he could muster and got up.

"You'll be sorry for this, *indio de mierda*," he said and left.

Rocco watched from the door until he saw Silvio get into his jeep and blast off at breakneck speed.

When he returned his attention to the room, he saw that Coral was no longer on the bed. She had found a shawl and was covering her torn clothes.

"Rocco," Stefan said. "I should not risk sounding impatient, but I could do without these bindings."

"I have a pocket knife," Rocco said, and cut him loose.

Both Coral and Stefan embraced him and thanked him. Rocco seemed flustered about being the recipient of such profuse gratitude.

Then he said something that confounded the other two.

"No need to thank me," he told them. "I'm just returning the favour."

When he realised his words had confused them even more, he added, "Some time ago Josefa told me the *señora* had been very kind to her. She didn't explain. She just said the *señora* had been very kind."

"I don't remember," Coral said. "It must have been of no importance."

Rocco picked up the gun from the floor, unloaded it, and gave the gun and the bullets to Stefan. "Hang on to this," he said. "You never know when you might need it."

Then he collected his rifle and his knife and walked to the door. Just before he left, he turned and smiled at them.

"*Vaya con Dios,*", he said.

EIGHTEEN

The Sadness Within

The following morning Coral met Stefan at the lobby of the hotel *Los Laureles*, in Miraflores.

"I'll come with you to the station," she had said and he had agreed.

He settled his account and they took a taxi to the station. He was carrying one small suitcase and a book.

"What are you reading?" she asked.

"Sartre," he told her. "I'm trying to understand what existentialism is all about."

"I think I have a clue."

"Do you?"

"From reading the French newspaper, *Le Monde.*"

"What is it?"

"A philosophical theory that places the individual as responsible for his own development...

or something to that effect."

"Makes sense."

The taxi drove through crowded streets, then moved onto the highway.

Stefan took Coral's hand and kissed it. "So you see," he said, "I even need you to interpret what I read."

At the station they walked up and down the crowded platform. There was nothing so lonely as a train station filled with strangers. And yet, a great weight was taken from Coral when she realised she did not know any of them.

No stares. No reporters. No gossip columnist. No chit-chat. Only the vivid sense of loneliness that would invade her when he left.

"Certain things rob you of your serenity," Coral said.

"Such as?" he asked.

"Sadness."

Stefan placed his hands on her shoulders and looked into her eyes.

"Coral," he said. "I have asked you to come with me. I have begged you to come with me. I have told you that I love you. I have purchased an airline ticket for you. But I can't force you to do what you're not willing to do."

"I would follow you to the end of the earth," she

told him. "But I can't walk out on Aurelio. It would destroy him." She paused a moment, then added, "I don't expect you to understand."

He held her tightly and touched his lips to the top of her head.

"I understand," he said.

At that moment a loud whistle announced the impending arrival of the train.

There it was. The whistle and the train had come together. She was unprepared for the arrival. So soon. Too soon. She no longer wished to let him go. She clung to the hope that some miracle would keep him from leaving. But that miracle was hers to perform; and she was powerless to do so, powerless to hold him back.

He took her in his arms and held her tightly, for a long time. When at last they separated, he turned away and boarded the train.

"Stefan," she called.

He appeared at the third window and waved at her. She waved back as the train began to move; slowly at first, then faster and faster.

Standing at the edge of the platform, like a soldier who has returned from another world, she waved to him and kept waving. Only then did she realise that she was waving at a train that was no longer there.

Epilogue

Epilogue

EPILOGUE

Frances Larsen had a worried look on her face as she watched her son, Stefan, coming down the stairs to join her at the breakfast table.

He looked pale, sombre and frightfully thin. When she had voiced her concern and asked if he had lost weight, he had dismissed the question saying he didn't think so.

"Morning, darling," she said.

"Morning, Mother."

She served him a cup of coffee.

"Colombian," she said. "Your favourite."

He raised the cup to his lips, then put it down again.

"I got the croissants at the French bakery."

"Great," he said, but did not touch them; he just gazed out of the window to where two swans were gliding on the pond beyond her garden.

"That chap from The Daily Telegraph called again," she told him. "He wants to know if you're covering the Syrian conflict."

"I'm not," Stefan said. "I told them to get

somebody else."

Frances did not insist. It was evident that something was terribly wrong. Whatever it was would remain his own affair for the moment.

But it was not in her nature to relinquish the struggle so easily.

"Stefan," she said. "Sometimes we're greatly troubled over things that don't matter, while ignoring what really counts."

"This is not the case, Mother," he told her. "I know what counts, but I'm not able to do anything about it."

She knew then that his heart was broken. She dismissed her need to do her best for him. Her best would not be enough, nothing would be. A broken heart was difficult to mend. She was the living proof that pain and anguish were huge burdens on the soul. Those afflicted would try in vain to cultivate indifference.

Should she urge Stefan to overcome what troubled him or persuade him to forget? Unable to decide, she said nothing.

She finished her coffee and picked up her mobile. As she checked her messages, she exclaimed, "Good Heavens!"

"What is it?" Stefan asked.

"You remember Aurelio Fernandez-Concha?

The gentleman you met in Lima."

"Of course. What about him?"

"He died three days ago. Heart attack. There is a Mass for him, today, at the Cathedral in Lima according to this e-mail from Professor Greene."

"May I see the message?"

She gave it to him. There was something about his face that puzzled her. She did not herself see anything so very shocking about the news. Sad, of course, but not particularly distressing. The curtain had fallen on a man who was neither young nor the object of affection to anyone but his own family.

When he spoke again, Stefan's voice was urgent and strong.

"Mother," he said. "Will you call British Airways and get me the first available flight from London to Lima?"

She gave him a long, appraising stare. She wondered evidently if this request had anything to do with the pattern of his reflections – those he had shared with her and those which had remained unknown.

"From London to Lima," she repeated. "Interesting."

"Think so?"

"The little I know of human nature, I have

learned in the sober comfort of the obvious."

"That's me? The obvious?"

"Not you. Your heart. But I won't ask you why you're now in pursuit of that which was not worth finding only a moment ago."

"A moment ago was a lifetime away. Rather difficult to explain."

"I'd be a damned fool if I didn't understand," she said, as she picked up the telephone and called British Airways.

* * *

Coral tied Monsieur Brown to a spindly poplar, then walked across a path that was choked with grass and moss, around a large pacay whose trunk was covered by ivy. Nature had its way with vegetation, as it did with people – or anything else for that matter.

A cloud passed over the sun and the fog took over again. Dense. Robbing the world of colour, turning it a dismal grey.

What now? she thought, then walked over to a weeping willow and sat down with her back against the trunk.

She was exhausted. For some reason she had expected herself to be stronger, perhaps from some mistaken notion that grief was likely to disperse, no matter how real.

But such a thing had not happened. Sorrow had invaded her with a breathless force, jolting memories, preventing her from regaining a certain calm, whatever a certain calm might be.

She knew, from looking in the mirror, that her eyes were red and her face blotchy from all those tears. Her black clothes were dismal and unbecoming, and her blond hair, pulled back and tied with a black ribbon, might have inspired a charcoal-grey drawing of a young widow, bleak and mournful in tone.

A great lump came in her throat and her eyes filled with tears as she recalled the events of the last four days.

Tuesday had dawned drizzly and cold, with dense fog. Xi had served their breakfast indoors – a bowl of porridge and jasmine tea for Aurelio, toast and coffee for her.

"Awful day," she had said. "Do you have to go to work?"

"I'm afraid so," Aurelio had answered. "Silvio is in Ancón with his family. Someone has to run the office."

Then he had embarked on a dissertation about world poverty and its social consequences. It was only a hypothesis, but, wouldn't life be easier if people were all rich or all poor? And if that were the case, would it be possible to reconcile certain elements that were in turmoil?

"Am I boring you, my dear?"

"Of course not."

Those were the last words they ever said to each other, except goodbye.

Two hours later, his secretary, Prunella, had found him slumped over his desk. She had known at once that there was nothing anyone could do for him. Dr. Martinez had issued the death certificate. Heart attack.

The Mass at the Cathedral had been sombre but beautiful, overflowing with family members, friends, dignataries and ordinary people from all over South America.

But nothing from Stefan. No telephone call. No telegram. No e-mail. No flowers. Nothing.

Monsieur Brown stamped his foot on the ground and gave a loud neigh. Coral raised her head to find out what had attracted his attention.

That was when she saw him.

He was walking away from the main house, headed towards the path that led to the guest cottage.

She took a deep breath, her heart thumping in her chest, a smile breaking on her lips.

"Stefan," she cried.

She got up and began running towards him. He saw her and began to run as well. Their coming together was unlike anything they had ever known.

He picked her up and held her tightly against him.

"I came as soon as I heard," he said.

A pale sun had begun to shine through the *neblina*. Monsieur Brown nibbled blades of grass. And a sparrow flew past them into the willow, carrying a bit of straw.